Ron Arends
12-10-06

Grandpa Grouper
The Fish with Glasses

Created and Written by Don Arends

Illustrated by Neelam

One morning at sunrise,

the mini-sub *Zodiac* crept up on the coral kingdom.
Dr. Sylvia Earle was searching for Grandpa Grouper,
King of the Coral Reef, the fish with glasses.

Where is Grandpa Grouper?

3

Dr. Sylvia Earle aimed her underwater floodlight.

How does Dr. Earle steer
the submarine?

As a "cat of the sea," Grandpa Grouper
was very curious. "What's that bright light?"
he wondered, coming out of his cave.

Grandpa Grouper swam right inside the sub's collecting globe! Some of his friends from the reef followed him.

Which fish is the smallest?

"Wow!"

Dr. Earle reported to her team above. "I've caught the grouper and he is the biggest one I've ever seen. He is wearing a crown and glasses!"

The radio team on the ship above laughed. "What a catch for the Blue Island Aquarium!" said the captain.

How does the team talk to each other?

"What's happening?" asked Posty Seahorse.
"This could be fun!" Jane Angelfish said.
"Where are we going?" asked Roper Trumpet.

"It looks like we are on our way to the aquarium," sighed Grandpa Grouper, as the coral reef disappeared behind them.

8

How many fish are in the globe?

Blue Island
Aquarium

9

Soon Grandpa Grouper and his friends were swimming and playing in their new home.

Grandpa Grouper became the new star of the Visitor's Show. Every day people came from all over to see him and catch his wink.

Which eye does he wink?

Everyone at the Blue Island Aquarium loved Grandpa Grouper – except Calvin Triggerfish.

Calvin Triggerfish was the star before
Grandpa Grouper came to the aquarium,
and he wanted to be the star of the show again.
"I'll show that old grouper a thing or two,"
mumbled Calvin.

He swam into Grandpa Grouper and bumped
him with his hammer-hard nose.
Off fell Grandpa Grouper's glasses and crown.

"Oh, no!" Grandpa Grouper cried
as his favorite things fell between
the coral and the rocks.

Grandpa Grouper was too big
to get his glasses and crown. His friends tried
to help. "Sorry, I can't reach your glasses and crown,
Grandpa Grouper," said Roper Trumpet.
"I can't get past the fire coral."

Where are the glasses and the crown?

14

Everyone was worried Grandpa would
never get his glasses and crown back!
Then Posty Seahorse said, "I'll try."

Posty Seahorse, who was

small enough to swim through the fire coral, said, "Sorry, Grandpa, it's too dangerous to reach them. They are in front of Harry Eel's cave."

"You know Harry gobbles up everything that swims by!"

Which animal does Posty look like?

Next, Buddy the big red sand crab tried.
"I can bury myself in the sand, crawl under the
glasses, and pull them out," he offered bravely.

"Go get 'em, Buddy!" cheered all the fish
in the aquarium.

18

Jane Angelfish distracted Harry Eel. Buddy Redcrab crawled under the sand. He quickly grabbed the glasses with one claw and the crown in the other.

Where is Harry Eel?

Buddy placed the glasses and crown back on top of Grandpa Grouper's head.

"Hooray!" All the fish cheered while Calvin sneered nearby.

What does Buddy have for his hands?

Suddenly, Harry Eel darted out of his cave after Calvin.
"Watch out!" Grandpa Grouper shouted, quickly pushing Calvin out of the way of the hungry eel and saving his life!

Although Grandpa Grouper liked being the star of the aquarium, he wanted to return home to the coral reef. Calvin, now Grandpa's newest best friend, asked to join him.

"When the aquarium closes for the night," Grandpa told his friends, "we'll escape through the feeding door."

Where is the
feeding door?

23

At eight o'clock the aquarium closed.
Most of the lights were turned off.
Grandpa Grouper and his friends put the
escape plan into action. Billy, the wide manta ray,
blocked the water drain, filling up
the aquarium to its ceiling.

Where is the clock?

Buddy floated up to open the feeding door with his claws.

When the door popped open, water flooded the aquarium and pushed Grandpa's friends out into the bay.

What fish is too big to get out the door?

26

Calvin Triggerfish
led the escape through the
underwater channels and past
dangerous razor sharp rocks.

"I'm glad you are with us,"
said Grandpa Grouper.
"You have a tough nose."

27

"Hooray!"

sang the fish as they swam home
to freedom in the coral kingdom.
Twinkle Starfish pointed north
so they wouldn't get lost.

28

As they arrived, sunbeams
highlighted the beautiful underwater colors.
Everyone joined in a big welcome home party,
and the fish wiggle danced with joy.

Can you wiggle dance?

Grandpa Grouper was happy to be home with his friends playing hide and seek. Once again, he was "King of the Coral Reef" ready for another sea life adventure!

How many fish can you find ?

The End

First Edition 2006
Text by Don Arends
Illustrations by Neelam

Published by:
Mission Manuscripts, Inc.
1000 Jorie Boulevard
Oak Brook, IL 60523 -2293
www.missionmanuscripts.com

ISBN: 0-9768880-0-9

Dedicated to my families, their grandchildren, friends and traveling teachers; proofreading help from my eight-year-old Oregon roping buddy, Cord Damuth; Executive Secretary, Kathy Hill.

Printed in the United States of America with the assistance of BooksjustBooks.com